# The Joy Behind Sorrow

Written by:
Michael P. Mark Jr.

Cadmus Publishing
www.cadmuspublishing.com

Published by Cadmus Publishing
www.cadmuspublishing.com
Port Angeles, WA

ISBN: 978-1-63751-073-5

# INTRODUCTION

First of all, I would like to thank everyone who supported the production of this book. This collection of poems was inspired by my true inner thoughts as well as the thoughts of others whom have shared certain experiences with me. In order to understand what it is that I am trying to convey, you must first be able to understand who you are and realize that art is abstract.

At times I wake up in the middle of the night with words on my mind that turn into poems. Ironically enough I don't consider myself a poet even though I write poetry. However, I am a fan of philosophy. Reading this book will get you thinking, but what you'll be thinking about depends on you. You may read my poems and feel that they are coming from a dark place; maybe they are or maybe they aren't. Remember, where there is darkness there is light. Without one there wouldn't be the other. The key word is abstract.

I often question myself and wonder how it is that my mind can produce such work. It could be that my mind isn't producing this work at all because it's within my heart. I was actually scared to share this collection of poems with the public.

I gathered the courage to put this collection out there because I realize that maybe my poems could help to inspire someone. The best thing for someone to do in life is to give, for in that act you also receive without expecting to.

As I have been inspired by many, my only hope is to be an inspiration to others. Let's keep love in our hearts, for there is enough hate in this world. Thank you for taking the time out to read this collection. With that being said, I hope that you enjoy.

"Follow your bliss and the universe will open doors
for you where there were only walls."

-Joseph Campbell

# Contents

Illuminate your life

# False Deity

As the Angels pulled me down
The demons pulled me up
At a stand still
Yet still I stand
Nevertheless it was never ending
Yet it ended
The sins cast into the sea of forgetfulness
Never to return nor see the light of day
You say lay it at the cross
Yet you have crossed me
The one that you took
Would've never been taken
Where there is truth there are also lies
I've danced with God
Is that the same as dancing with the devil

# THE BLINDING LIGHT

Don't look up at the sun
Is what she told me
But I chose to
Guess that's why I was blinded by you
You help put my heart back together
You left me heartbroken
I looked in your eyes and I was blinded by the light
I couldn't see the darkness in your eyes
I can't believe you turned out to be so cold
Guess that everything that glitters isn't gold

# Memories

Four walls closing in on me
In the dark
I still can see
I've forgotten all my memories
I forgot all of my memories
I don't know if
I will be
A long lost memory
A lost memory

# Songs That Keep You Here With Me

Driving against the wind
With my pride by my side
In the name of love
Down on main street
In search of the place
Where the streets have no name
In hopes that I shall find that beautiful day
But I still haven't found what I'm looking for
So I turn the page
Trying to find out what happened that day
April 20th

# Omen

I awoke in a labyrinth of emptiness
Yet I was never truly awake
Trying to find something
Where there is nothing
Yearning for a sign
Yet there aren't any signs
For that which I am yearning for

# ATTAINABLE UNATTAINABLE GOALS

The love that I lost once ago
Shall I ever retrieve
One must know sorrow in order to obtain happiness
For happiness is the sorrow that drives my pain
As I look down I see that which is unattainable
For below me is where I want to be
Yet I am unable to reach

✦

# Omega

Shall thou ever discover thine destiny
What art thou destined to be
The destination of one
Is it the same as one destination
Where what who when why
What art thou destined to be
Shall thou ever discover thine destiny

# BURNING DESIRES

The anger inside
Only to be quenched
By the desire
To be cast into the fire
That which produces the flames
Of iniquity, shame, and despair
To look beyond
Is to look before
Before there was…

# Am I Here

As I purge
In the flames of the fire
From the abyss
Of everlasting pain, torture, and torment
I am here
But yet I am not
Lost love
Love lost
What was
Is
Will be

# BROKEN

So broken
That I hate to even feel
For to feel
Is to lose
Everything
That is good
Within me

# FORBIDDEN

Never could I have ever imagined that I
Could have everything I've ever wanted
Yet have nothing at all
She is that of my desire
However it cannot be
As time and life would have it
Love
Doesn't always prevail
In essence
She is my melancholy
As well as
My zenith

# KEEPING HOPE ALIVE

As I enter the coldness of dawn
With remnants of the night before
I realize that once the night is young
Young is the night no more
I close my eyes
For they have been open too long
In hopes that the tune I hear
Will be the tune of a different song

# How Long Will It Ever

The reflection of the sun off the pure white
How long will it last
The last breath from the breath of life
How long will it last
Time ever seemingly so limitless
How long will it last
Thou shalt not
Will it ever last

# THOUGHTS FROM A HAPPY PLACE

Beyond the light
That is
Beyond the light
I find comfort
In the darkness
Of the light
In peril I lay
In peril I stay
Still I await
I pray for that day

# Siren

With my eyes wide shut
My heart has been broken
Picking up the pieces
Of lies
Which lies
Between the eyes
Of the one
Who drowned in tears
In fear of the truth

# TRUE FREEDOM

Water from the fountain of youth
Fire from a burning bush
The hanging gardens
My history
Drowned in the waters of my oppressors
Burned alive
Only my body
Never my spirit
Hung from the tree of racism
I can still see the blood on the leaves
Freedom yet I am not free from doom
Bars keep me no more
For my mind is the universe

+

# Changes In The Unforeseen

The soul of a monster
Becomes the soul of a man
Cast in the sea of blood
He who envisions that which is not seen
Shall envenom that which surrounds him
Of the world
Of the unknown

# THAT WHICH HAS BEEN LOST

Surrounded by souls
But yet I am alone
Still and buried
In the ashes of perished memories
Neither life nor death can
Account for…
What's been forgotten

# The First Time

You have captured my heart
For I have been captivated by you
As if I'm in a universe that is parallel to my own
As if the stars have aligned
As if I am the universe
And the universe I
You came at a time when love was lost to me
For the love I found before you wasn't love
How could I lose that which was never found
Like a virgin

# HER PAIN

I never asked to be here
You forced me to
All I ever wanted…
A relationship with you
Why would you have me
Just to leave me…
All alone in this cold dark world
The pain it took for me to be here
Doesn't equate the pain it took for me to stay here
Three sheets to the wind
For I know no other way
To deal with the pain shame and torture that is…
Burning deep within my soul my spirit
Within the depths of my despair
Will you ever

# The Regret of Survival

The sorrow of surviving that which you didn't
Live life with no regrets
However I cannot
Was your time the right time
How soon is soon enough
Not my time or have I escaped
I keep on living
As you live on in my heart

# Acknowledgements

I would like to thank everyone who has made an impact on my life, be it negative or positive. You all have inspired me.

Also I would like to express my gratitude to the following people for their love, support and contributions to the creation of this book:

To my dear Mother: Thank you for always being there for me as well as your unwavering support and faith in me. I appreciate everything you've done for me in life as well as for the creation of this book. I love you dearly.

To my Father: In life and in death you have shown me what it is to be a man and a father. I have been deeply saddened by your untimely death. However, I cherish all of our memories. Through you I have life. Through me you live on. Words can't express how much I miss you. I love you, Dad.

To my brother Byron: I love you and thank you for your love and support.

To my brother Baby: Words cannot express my gratitude. Thank you for how you've stepped up. I'm proud of you. You have me the boost that I needed. I love you so much, bro.

Uncle Andy: I love you, Unc. Thanks for always being a man of your word. Thank you for being there for me. We will soon do great things together.

Aunt Geraldine: Thank you for your beautiful letters, words of encouragement, and support. I hold many cherished memories with you. I love you, Aunty Gerri.

Aunt Betty: I love you and I am truly grateful for your love and support.

My dear cousin Jolene: Thank you for your love and support. I am truly grateful to have you in my life and I truly appreciate how you've helped me get through my father's untimely passing. You are the closest person to me that keeps me connected to my father. I love you and I miss you. I hope to be in London soon.

To my since day one friends: Angel, Jov, Don, Pancho, Jay, Dario, Miguel, and of course Donte. There isn't any amount of money that equals what your friendship means to me. Priceless. Thank you, I love and appreciate you all.

To my new friends that I've met during my journey: Troy, Trev, Banga, Yusef, TDDA, Twizz, Rockinton, Mike, Ox, Scoot, J. Silva, Jeffrey, Musa, A.D., Budda (everything fine on vine), Sweets (yes now), Rapp, Nick, Quan, Moncho, Q, Brody (G), Pretty, Fluke, Nine, BARLOW, WAHID, Audi, D.S., Nat. I love y'all, we are our own brotherhood.

Steph: You already know how much you mean to me. I love you, and thanks for always doing right by me.

Angie, Rita, Luis, Luisito, Pito: You guys will always be my family. I love you all.

Dona Francis: Te quiero mucho y gracias por tus oraciones.

Neysha: I truly appreciate everything you've done for me including uplifting my spirits. Unexpectedly you have made a huge impact on my life. I love you and I'll always be there for you. "Sweet Dreams."

Shoutout to Lexi and Adrianna. I'm glad that I met y'all. I love your energy.

My top five: You all have really been there for me even when I couldn't be there for myself. I love y'all to death, and thanks for keeping it real.

To my haters a.k.a. motivators: Thank you, for you have fueled my energy for greatness.

To the people that I do care about but failed to mention, I don't love you any less but at some point it has to end. (lol)

Lastly, my beautiful daughter Michaela, I love you with all of my being. Without you, I would've given up a long time ago. You are the best thing that's ever happened to me. I'm so proud of you. You inspire me to be better. As you make me proud, I want to make you proud of me. I'll do my best to be a proper father to you. Thank you for being my perfect daughter. You have the most beautiful smile. Daddy loves you, princess.

"Family is all we got."

-R.W.

Thank you, Big Sis, I love you so much. You're the best big sister anyone can ever have.

# ABOUT THE AUTHOR

Michael P. Mark, Jr. is a man who sees the world through a multilateral lens. He's full of thought-provoking questions, as demonstrated in some of his work. His ultimate goal is to get others to think and allow themselves to view the world in ways they aren't accustomed to. Mr. Mark is currently in a state of thought.

He is the proud recipient of the 2021 St. Jude Children's Research Hospital Appreciation Award. He always strives to help others and leads a life full of love. Mr. Mark is also student at Quinnipiac University where he studies crime and society, sociology, and sociology of economics. He also successfully completed the Paralegal Studies course with distinction from Blackstone Career Institute.

His proudest accomplishment: his beautiful, intelligent light of his life daughter, Michaela Mark.

www.ingramcontent.com/pod-product-compliance
Lightning Source LLC
Chambersburg PA
CBHW060602100726
47907CB00005B/1478